BROOK IROQ WASHINGTON PUBLIC LIBRARY
P.O. BOX 155 100 W. MAIN ST.
BROOK. IN 47922

SO-AIE-908

by Lea Taddonio   illustrated by Mina Price

Head over Heels

First Fight

Spellbound

An Imprint of Magic Wagon
abdopublishing.com

To PB &J, my favorite combo —LT

For Corinne & Tori —MP

abdopublishing.com

Published by Magic Wagon, a division of ABDO, PO Box 398166,
Minneapolis, Minnesota 55439. Copyright © 2017 by Abdo
Consulting Group, Inc. International copyrights reserved in all
countries. No part of this book may be reproduced in any form
without written permission from the publisher. Spellbound™ is a
trademark and logo of Magic Wagon.

Printed in the United States of America, North Mankato, Minnesota.
102016
012017

**THIS BOOK CONTAINS
RECYCLED MATERIALS**

Written by Lea Taddonio
Illustrated by Mina Price
Edited by Heidi M.D. Elston
Art Directed by Candice Keimig
Series lettering and graphics from iStockphoto

Publisher's Cataloging-in-Publication Data

Names: Taddonio, Lea, author. | Price, Mina, illustrator.
Title: First fight / by Lea Taddonio ; illustrated by Mina Price.
Description: Minneapolis, MN : Magic Wagon, 2017 | Series: Head over heels ; Book 3
Summary: Lola Jones has strong feelings for star basketball player C.J Kline. But when
    her big brother finds out, the couple may be torn apart for good.
Identifiers: LCCN 2016947642 | ISBN 9781624041947 (lib. bdg.) | ISBN 9781624022548
    (ebook) | ISBN 9781624022845 (Read-to-me ebook)
Subjects: LCSH: High school students--Juvenile fiction. | Best friends--Juvenile fiction. |
    Interpersonal relationships--Juvenile fiction. | Human behavior--Juvenile fiction.
Classification: DDC [Fic]--dc23
LC record available at http://lccn.loc.gov/2016947642

Table
of
Contents

Keeping a Secret

I'm on my bed listening to my **FAVORITE** song, thinking about last night's date with C.J. His **cute** smile. How good he smelled. The way his hand felt PRESSED against mine. I slam a **PILLOW** over my face and giggle.

My door OPENS. "What're you doing?" My big brother, Joseph, gives me a **strange** look.

"Ever hear of **KNOCKING**?" I ask.

"What's so *funny*?" he says.

6

"Your face." I stick out my **TONGUE**.

He **frowns**. "Get up. We're leaving in five minutes."

Tonight the Washington High **WARCATS** play the Potter Hill *Pirates*. The Pirates aren't a good basketball team, but they have the **BEST** drum line in the state. I'm nervous.

"I'm **READY**," I yell, but Joseph is already outside. My phone buzzes with a text, and I forget to breathe.

It's him.

C.J.

"Calm down," I whisper. But my heart slams against my ribs.

C.J

Want to know a secret?

I write back: okay.

C.J

I can't stop thinking about you.

My cheeks hurt from my *smile* while I type back:
Focus on winning tonight's game, Hot Shot.

C.J

I've got to tell Joseph about us.
He has to know.

My mouth falls open. What's C.J *thinking*?

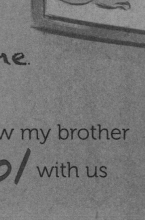

C.J's my brother's **BEST FRIEND**. He knows Joseph better than *anyone*. Even me.

Doesn't C.J know my brother will never be **cool** with us being . . .

What are we *anyway*?

C.J and I aren't boyfriend and girlfriend. We haven't even **kissed**. I've never **kissed** anyone. And **NEVER** will if Joseph has his way.

I pick up my phone to type **STOP** when the screen goes **BLACK**. Dead battery. Just my *luck*.

So Busted

The game was a **disaster**. The Warcats won, but I couldn't stay on **BEAT**. I kept staring at Joseph on the bench. It was hard to tell if he looked **mad**. Had C.J told him about our date? It made me feel **sick** not to know.

"**WHERE** was your head tonight, Lola?" the band director asks me.

"**Nowhere good,**" one of the other drummers mutters.

I'm not used to this. I am a girl who can **focus**. I have big *dreams* of becoming the best drummer in the school. What if I mess up everything because of **boy drama**?

"Sorry," I whisper. "I have a **headache**." Great. Not only am I a mess-up, I am a **LIAR**.

I wait for Joseph in the parking lot, looking at the ground. I don't want to talk to *anyone*.

"Lola?" That **DEEP** voice belongs to the cause of my **bad mood**.

"Good **GAME**, C.J.," I say.

"I haven't told Joseph yet,"
C.J says.

I turn around. *"For real?"*
Maybe there's still time to talk
SENSE into him.

"I want **YOU** to tell him," he says.

"Tell me what?" Joseph stands between us with a **TIGHT** look on his face.

What I Want

"What does my **little sister** need to tell me?" Joseph asks in a **LOW** voice.

I **SHRUG**. "No clue. He's just **messing** around. Right, C.J?"

"Yeah. Right." C.J gives a **strange** laugh, one that doesn't sound **funny**. "I guess there's nothing for me to do but go home." He *turns* around.

And that's when I know the **TRUTH**. If I say nothing, C.J will walk away. I'll *lose* my chance with him **FOREVER**.

He takes one step and then another.

"I **wonder** what's up with that guy tonight. We won the **GAME**." Joseph takes out his keys. "Want to get a **hamburger** on the way home?"

"Wait!" The word bursts from me.

Joseph's eyebrows **SMASH** together. He looks annoyed. "Did you forget something in the school?"

"I have to put this right." I turn and *RUN* after C.J. "Stop, C.J. *Please*."

C.J looks tired. "What is it, Lola?"

I take a **DEEP** breath. "I don't want to make my brother upset. He carries so much **STRESS** ever since Dad left. He feels like he has to look out for Mama and me. But I don't want to hide the truth. I have *feelings* for you."

C.J grins. "I have *feelings* for you too, Lola. I have for a **LONG** time."

"What's that you just said?" Joseph steps forward **looking** like he's ready to put a **FIST** in C.J's **MOUTH**.

"We want to be **together**," I say.

"No way." Joseph **shakes** his head at C.J. "**NOT** Lola. **NOT** my sister, man."

"It's not like that," C.J says.

"It's **EXACTLY** like that," Joseph shouts. "You could have any *girl* in the **CITY**." C.J **SHRUGS**. "Guess I've got *good* taste."

"She's not **ALLOWED** to *date* basketball players, and that's *FINAL*." Joseph steps forward, hands **CLENCHED**.

That's when I've had **ENOUGH**. It's time to go after what I *want*.

ch 4

This Is My Life

I step BETWEEN them and hold *out* my arms, keeping them apart. "Both of you need to **SHUT UP** and *listen*."

I hold up one finger. "**First**, I make decisions for *myself*. Joseph, you are my brother, and I love you, but this is my **LIFE**."

I raise another finger. "**Second**, I *should've* told you about C.J, but I didn't know what to say. This is all *new* to me. I needed time to **think** it over."

I hold up another finger. "**Third**, C.J, I'm *sorry* if I made you feel *dishonest*."

C.J takes my *hand*. "You aren't someone I want to hide."

"Good." Joseph *crosses* his arms. "My sister is *special*. She might make me crazy but **FAMILY** is **FAMILY**. She and my mom are all I have."

Hot *tears* burn my eyes.

C.J clears his throat. "You're my ***BEST FRIEND***. I won't do anything that ever disrespects your sister."

Hope **FILLS** my chest. "Does that mean you won't get **mad** if I spend time with C.J?" I ask.

"As long as you aren't **kissing** and **HUGGING** around me all the time." My brother makes a **face**.

C.J nods. "If that's the case, I want to **walk** her home."

Joseph is quiet for a few seconds. "**Yeah**. I see how it is. Be home by curfew, **Sis**."

C.J and I *walk* in silence for a block. "I don't like *fighting*," he says at last. "I'm glad we're at the **next** part."

"What's the next part?" I ask. He gives me a *wink*. "Making up."

BROOK IROQ WASHINGTON PUBLIC LIBRARY
P.O. BOX 155 100 W. MAIN ST.
BROOK, IN 47922